Lady Jay

By

Wayne Seaden

Chapter one

After three and a half hours driving, it was time to stop. We had left it too late in the day, to leave home and it was beginning to get dark.

We were supposed to be heading to a beer festival in Weymouth, but courtesy of some of our party running late, it put us somewhat behind.

After some time, we found this sleepy little village and proceeded to look for somewhere to stop. After much trying and the locals not really wanting to commit themselves to helping us, we finally found an old house. It looked over a hundred years old, the brickwork crumbling, the cement only just holding the building together. The windows had broken in a few places and all the others were gone completely, allowing the elements to enter and ravage the insides.

Our little group of friends were always quite bold in our adventures and would rarely shy away from doing something like this. But seeing this place in the fading light, started to change our way of thinking.

We got here around nine o'clock in the evening. There were four of us all together, Steven, Tony, Michael and me. Steve had been driving, as he had been to Weymouth before and knew what roads to take. The place looked quite cool, in a weird way. We knew this was going to be a weekend to remember, only, it was going to be for the wrong reasons.

We got out of the car and cautiously walked to the front door. We stopped on the front porch and paused.

It wasn't even locked and opened easily. There wasn't much light inside the house, but we could see just enough, to make out some oil lamps on the walls which Steve took upon himself to approach and light.

"Don't you think it would make sense to check and make sure there is no one here first, before we start walking around somebody else's house?" Michael asked.

"you really think someone would live in a shit hole like this" Steven replied.

As he said that, the light slowly filled the hallway to display the cold interior of another time. The interior was clearly dated and in dire need of some care. "if someone does live here, then they badly need to decorate, look at the state of this place, it's a mess". Tony remarked.

Steven turned to look at Tony in annoyance. "I don't care what the place looks like. It looks dry, so, as long as we can stay here and get some sleep until morning, what's the problem?".

He drew in a deep breath "HELLO!" he shouted out.

The sound rattled through the house and echoed loudly upstairs. "ANYONE HERE?" he shouted again.

Michael butted in quickly, he was always the one to defuse an argument. "ok, let's just go and have a look around "he said. "you never know, we may find something here ".

"thinking of doing some treasure hunting?" I jokingly replied.

"no, but you never know unless you look".

Steven laughed "you probably wouldn't know what to look for anyway". I turned to face them, "ok, if we are going to look around, then we must go together and not stray too far from the group. That way, if anything happens while we are looking, we can all help".

Tony shivered. "nice one Wayne, scare me more than I already am".

"sorry, but that's the way it is going to have to be, if we are to do this" I said back and gently squeezed his shoulder to reassure him.

I reached into my pocket and withdrew my cigarettes, offered them around and we made our way around the house. We started by heading upstairs. Bendy old things, the banisters were all cracked and full of woodworm and in places, parts of the bannister were missing.

They bent round to the right as we ascended the staircase, we could see, rusty nails protruding out of the boards in the steps. They creaked loudly as if to warn us of impending danger, but the curiosity in us was overpowering and we continued.

Once at the top of the stairs, I glanced back to the front door. It had closed shut, none of us heard it close. I turned back to see Steven staring at the door. "Did you shut the door when you came through?" I asked him. Steven must have been thinking the same thing. "I was just about to ask the same; I left the door open". He replied.

A vast space lay beneath us, the varnished wooden floor now covered in decades of dust, pieces of wallpaper and leaves that had been blown in from the shattered windows.

By the door was an arch of clean floor, where the door had swung closed and swept the floor clean. A moderate breeze was gently swaying through the house. Warm air was coursing through the upstairs from a far bedroom. From the landing, we could see which room the wind was coming from.

The door was wide open, allowing the wind to barrel its way down the landing and down the stairs to the floor below.

Along the walls, were a number of aged pictures. Some clinging to the wall for dear life and hanging in place by a thread, the fixings barely holding. Steven had remarked at how the man of the house had to of been really bad at DIY and his wife would have been proud of his abilities.

One of the pictures, was a family picture. Like the others, it was aged and faded, but you could clearly see the image of a man and a woman with a little boy standing to the side of the lady.

We proceeded to walk towards the open doorway not realising what was going to happen.

The atmosphere was chilling, despite the warm breeze cascading through. Approaching the room, we paused. All four of us stood in the doorway staring into the black void of the room. Only a few small beams of light projected in through the window. They cast small circles to the far corner of the room like a wartime searchlight, pinpointing an aircraft in the sky. One of the areas, illuminated a small pile of pictures. I was slightly confused. The house had been empty, for years and yet there were still belongings, scattered about here and there.

 This made me ask myself a number of questions. 'who would leave their belongings? why didn't they return for them? And why hadn't the place been pulled down?'.

Steven took a torch out of his pocket and pressed the switch. A beam of light shot into the room. He swung it from side to side, scanning the floor. Then raising it slightly and began to scan the walls.

"don't go in Steve!" Tony called out. He was feeling scared, as was I.

"let me go in first" Steven said back "I'm not bothered" and he took a step forward. Tony started to shake, "I don't think it's a good idea, there is something in there" he pleaded.

"don't be stupid, there is nothing in here, there is nothing in this house. You need to grow some balls "Steven replied sarcastically.

Before Tony could object to his comment, Steven had taken a few more steps forward into the room. His work boots thumped onto the floor, as he walked further in. The sound began to echo down the landing and throughout the house". He stopped in the centre of the room and just stood there motionless and speechless, staring out of the window.

We cautiously followed, pausing after every step.

Michael was the first to voice his fear. "ok, so there is nothing in this room but old papers and pictures. Let's look in the next room". And he turned to face the door and possibly his only escape route.

He didn't have to say it again, by the time he had turned to face the door, Tony had already placed himself in the doorway. I looked at Steve "are you coming, or are you going to just stand there staring out the window?". All I got in return for my question, was a low humming noise, which I assumed was the wind forcing itself through the cracks in what was left of the windows.

I walked towards the door and as I passed through it, I turned back to look at Steve "If you're going to stay there all night, the least you could do, is say so and not just stand there saying nothing". That was when I thought I heard him mumble something, it sounded like he agreed. This gave me a little confidence. Whatever put him into a trance, was wearing off and he was going to turn around and follow us out of the room. So, I turned myself back around and followed Tony and Michael towards the next room.

Without warning, the door slammed behind me with Steve still inside the room. It slammed with force, echoing through the entire house. It was like a bomb going off, we could feel the vibrations rattling the floorboards. I could swear that the house was going to collapse around us. Michael spun round to face me. "is Steve still in there?" he asked. I turned; Steve was nowhere to be seen. "he must be" and I trotted back to the door.

I grabbed hold of the doorknob, it was icy cold, making me let go with surprise. I regained my grip and tried to push open the door. It wouldn't move. Placing my full weight against the door, I tried thrusting my way through, we could hear the door creaking, every time I made contact. Being in the state it was, we couldn't believe the door was holding strong. "you better not be taking the micky out of us Steve". I took a few steps back and ran full pelt at the door. Pain ripped into my shoulder as contact was made, but still the door held.

Suddenly, the door slowly creaked open.

"Where the hell is, he? he's gone!" Michael yelled. In the dim light of the room, it was obvious that Steve had gone. By now, we were all on edge. Not surprising really, Steve was there one minute, gone the next. He hadn't passed us on the landing, which he would have done, had he followed us out of the room.

"oh shit, what's happening in this place? I'm not going to take this, I'm going back to the town and staying at the B&B, where at least I won't go missing" Tony shouted. By now he was getting hysterical with fear, I had never seen someone this scared before and that was making Michael and I feel worse at the same time.

I took hold of Tony's shoulder "we cannot leave without Steve".

Tony glanced at me with an angry expression on his face.

"I have the feeling; he won't be coming back with us anyway" Michael called out.

"why?" I asked, as I looked into the centre of the room where Steve had been standing.

Michael shrugged his shoulders. "Tony is right, I think there is something in this house with us and it's not good".

"how do you know that?" I smirked. My mind was starting to unhook itself from the reality we knew.

Michael placed his hands inside his jacket pockets "a couple of things really, one; while Steve was in the other room staring out the window, we had made our way out and towards the other room, right?". I found his attitude quite amusing; he had gone into inspector Morse mode. "yes" I replied giggling to myself. I myself was trying to figure out how Steve could have possibly crept past us, without any of us seeing him.

"was he actually looking out of the window? look!" and he pointed to a picture in the wall, placed between both windows.

"didn't you notice that picture before we left? I did and it looks like it was done yesterday". It was something I hadn't really noticed previously, but now it was pointed out; I could see it clearly.

"all the pictures in this place look ancient but that one. Two: when you finally broke the door down, there was something else in that room apart from Steve. The door flew open, I saw some weird mist shoot out of the room, through the window and it was definitely not Steve".

Tony started to shake "that's it, I'm getting out of here".

"What's the matter now Tony?" I pleaded.

Tony pointed up to the ceiling above where Steve had been standing.

We all stared at the middle of the room. There appeared to be a large stain on the ceiling.

"Yes, and that's supposed to be?" Michael replied.

Tony bravely took a step forward and reached his arm up and extended his forefinger and touched it. Whatever it was, it was wet.

As his finger pulled away, it dripped onto him. Tony stared at his finger and then to the droplet on his arm.

"it's blood! its blood! "he shouted.

I approached Tony and looked up at the patch. I then did the same, not wanting to believe what Tony had just said. I reached up and touched it. My finger slid along with ease. Whatever it was, it was wet, thick and surprisingly, it was warm. As I brought my hand back down, I could see the red on my fingertip appear as my vision focused on it. It was definitely blood and it was soaking into the plaster.

"it can't be Steve's blood, surely" Michael called out from the doorway.

"no, don't be stupid, of course not" I replied.

"how could it possibly be his blood? If he cut himself, I'm sure we would have heard him, you know what he's like".

Steve was the type of person, who would let you think he was tough and then at the first sight of blood, he would run a mile in the opposite direction.

Tony yelped like a Yorkshire terrier "if that's the case, where is he? He didn't come past us and he didn't go out of the window. You can clearly see that and there are no other doors or cupboards he could hide in".

I agreed, Steve could not have gotten past us, and he certainly didn't fall out either of the windows.

They were two large bay windows, that overlooked the side of the property. The aged wooden frames had now started rotting away. The glass itself had thick veins of lead running through them in intricate patterns.

The only parts of the windows Steve could have tried to get out of, were the very tops and they were way too small for his eighteen stone of weight to squeeze through.

"well, we had better try looking for him, but we are not going to split up, we must stay together" I said.

Then, I realised something that Michael had said earlier.

"what has Steve going missing got to do with that picture anyway?" I said, walking over to the picture hanging between the windows.

It was a similar, one to the one we had seen earlier on the landing. It was clean, unfaded. The people in it were also the same. They were wearing the same clothes. Michael joined me by the picture.

"Look at it, it looks old, but it hasn't faded like the others have".

Tony also approached and stood by my side. He was starting to get some of his composure back.

"I've just checked all of the photos in this room. Most of them have faded. Some are completely blank. This one looks new".

I was stunned. Tony was right. Most of them had faded and yet this picture was in immaculate condition. all I could ask myself was why?

Michael pointed a finger at the picture "is that a plaque above there?"

I had to focus a little but in amongst the peeling wallpaper, there was a small brass plate a few inches above the picture. The plate was grubby, so I gave it a rub with the cuff of my sleeve to reveal the words underneath.

LADY JAY AND PETER ;1896 were written in bold letters.

I faced the other two. "it sounds strange, but maybe this photo has got something to do with all this, but I'm not wasting my time looking at art when Steve could be in danger or worse. I suggest, if he's about this house, then we better get looking for him" I said.

I then started walking towards the door. Michael quickly followed "where do we look first" he asked.

"the patch is on the ceiling, so I think we need to look for a hatch or a stairway that leads up to the attic, if that's blood, its coming from up there" I replied. So, we started walking down the landing checking room to room as we went. We opened door after door and peered inside. Some of the rooms had an icy chill. We put that down to the fact that those rooms had windows missing. Although it was midsummer, sometimes the evenings had a chill to them.

We reached the end of the landing and were confronted with two identical doors. Tony moved toward the door on the left, I grabbed the handle of the door on the right.

"this is the one" I called out.

"How do you know that?" Michael replied.

I stretched my sleeve over my hand and grabbed hold of the handle again "it's the same as the other door, its freezing". Tony shut his door and joined me and Michael.

I put my weight against the door and pressed the side of my head against it. If Steve was up there and injured, I should have surely heard him through the door. Michael and Tony stood there motionless, waiting in anticipation. I held my breath and listened. Nothing!

I pushed the handle down and slowly opened the door. It opened with some ease.

The room inside was darker than the others. The chill was there, the same as the room Steve had been in. The far corner was a lot darker than the rest of the room. Again, as with the others, wallpaper was peeling off the wall. However, this room was void of any pictures. All that was left in this room, was a small decaying rug by the window. Its edges frayed and a rip had coursed its way from one of the corners into the middle.

We walked into the room and things started to appear much lighter and clearer. The dark area in the corner became much more visible. "another door" Tony remarked. "how many rooms has this place got?".

In the corner was a narrow doorway, I wasn't sure if it led to another room or if it was just a cupboard. Suddenly the humming sound returned. We all became quite uneasy at hearing it again. Tony started to panic and was breathing heavily. Michael walked towards the door and reached out a hand to open it and pulled it back quickly.

"I don't like this; I'm going to get a torch from the car. I would feel much more comfortable if I can see better" Michael said, and he turned and started walking out of the room. Tony was right behind him. That made me panic, I was not staying in there on my own. So, like sheep following the herd, we walked out of the room towards the stairs and made our way out to the car.

Once at the car, Michael opened the boot and started rummaging through his toolbox. We watched as bags, jackets and supplies came flying out and onto the floor. "got it!" he calls out and suddenly the boot lights up with a brilliant white light. Turning round, Michael swung the torch back and forth, illuminating the trees. Branches were highlighted. They looked like they were reaching out for us with thin pointy fingers. The light beam swung along the footpath leading to the house.

Michael slammed the boot back down and started walking back to the house and leaving me and Tony in the darkness.

Suddenly Tony yelled, scaring me half to death. "Stop ".

Michael froze for a moment then turned to face me and Tony.

"what now?" he shouted back.

"you might want to wait for us" Tony replied.

"well, you might want to shift your arses then" and he turned back towards the house.

We picked up the pace in a bid to catch up with Michael. We finally caught up with him about six feet from the front door.

Michael was looking up at the second floor, sweeping the torch along the walls, room to room.

"I think we need to go round to this side of the house; the attic window is round that side" and he pointed the torch to the left and down towards the corner.

Tony was first to go round the corner of the building, as we approached the corner, we saw Tony standing and simply pointing upwards. He wasn't saying a word. He just pointed to the top of the house.

Michael was a little annoyed. "what is the matter now" he asked.

Tony brought his arm back to his body and thrust it upwards again "look! There is a light on up there". I looked up and I felt my sanity start to creep out of my head and drift away into the night. It was already clinging on by its sinews, but now, it was starting to let go. I knew I was going to have a struggle on my hands, if I was going to keep what sanity I had left.

Sure enough, up in the top window, a faded, yellow light was pulsing inside the attic.

It cast a dull beam onto the back footpath, creating images amongst the foliage of shrubs and overgrown grass and weeds.

"I am right in assuming that there weren't any lights on up there earlier?".

Tony dropped his arm down by his side "no there was not. The only light that was on, was on the landing. We didn't open the door to the attic, so no light would have come from the landing and through that window".

Michael agreed "that's definitely coming from that attic room. He must be in there".

Tony's courage started to leave him again. "can we just look around out here, I would feel much safer".

"grow some balls, will you!" Michael quipped and he started to head back round to the front of the house. As we walked, I thought I saw movement, it was only out of the corner of my eye, but I was certain there was someone standing in the window and looking down on us. I wasn't quite sure if I wanted to look up at the window or not, as the dancing lights on the floor were quite worrying. It was as if there was more than one person in the attic.

I called out to the other two, as they had now gained a few paces further than me. "I maybe speaking for myself, but I'm sure there is someone or something watching us. Can anyone feel it?".

Michael stopped, started to turn, then stopped. "I'm not sure I want to look; in case I see something, I do not want to see. I'm starting to get a little worried about this place and I just want to find Steve and get the hell out of here. Even if it does mean paying to stay in a bed and breakfast for what's left of the night".

He was right, we were all starting to lose control, something I didn't enjoy.

I skipped a few steps to catch up with them. "we cannot chicken out now. Do you really think that there's something up there, ready to cut your head off and use it as a football for the undead FA cup final? I don't think so".

Tony must have been starting to feel brave, as his next comment shocked me a little. "I'm sorry but I'm starting to think the same as Michael, nothing seems to be right with this place. Look what we have already seen".

"and what would that be? "I replied.

"Steve's disappearance, for one. One minute he was there, next minute he was gone, and that weird patch of blood appeared on the ceiling. Secondly, those two pictures. All the others showed their age, but them two. They looked like they were taken yesterday. Now there is the light from the attic. We were able to check all the rooms but the one with the attic door in. None of us could have possibly turned that light on as we have all been together, even when Steve vanished. If Steve is anywhere, that's where he will be".

Michael butted in "so if none of us turned the light on, who did?".

"if it wasn't Steve, then someone or something else is in there playing games with us" I replied.

"like what? I hope you are not saying that there is an axe murderer in there waiting to kill us, do you?".

"either that or the something else. I'm not psychic, but something is telling me, that something is amiss here".

Before we could clear the rear of the house, the torch flashed past what could have only been the back door. It appeared to look quite heavy, possibly oak, but it looked buckled and warped.

As we approached the torch showed more of the doorway. The varnish was peeling away and dropping to the floor, the wind carrying it away across the garden.

"what the hell is that?" Tony shouted, pointing at the door.

As Michael trained the torchlight onto the door handle, we could clearly see something dripping off the doorknob and onto the floor. On closer inspection, we could see that it was covered in blood. It was covered in it. Crimson fluid still moving over the doorknob and dripping onto the floor in slow movements and creating a slowly swelling puddle of blood on the aged floorboards of the back porch.

It was really strange, for a moment I thought that the house was possibly alive. That it had been hurt and its lifeblood was running out in a bid to escape its host.

Was it alive? Everything hadn't made much sense from the first moment we arrived here. Things were happening that made no sense and we had no idea what was causing them to happen.

"you don't think Steve came out this way, do you?"

"no way" I replied. "if Steve had of left that room, we would have known about it. We would have seen or heard him. Remember he's a big bloke".

Michael laughed. "courtesy of the beer and fry ups, Steve isn't easy to lose".

"ok. Well the light upstairs is still on and by the looks of the light, someone is still there. I would hazard a guess, that, that is where Steve is".

Tony looked confused. "but surely, if Steve is still upstairs, who's blood is that?".

Michael had found a rag on the floor and started to wipe the blood off the doorknob. He could feel the warmth still. "I don't really care who's blood it is or where it's come from, I just want to find Steve and get out of here".

Suddenly there was an ear-piercing scream. It came from all around us. None of us could tell if it was a male, female or some kind of animal. The sound was so twisted and contorted. As the sound subsided, it became more obvious as to where the scream originated from.

It came from inside the house.

Chapter two

We ran back to the front door. It was wide open. "Someone is definitely playing with us" Tony remarked as he grabbed hold of the door and started swinging it closed and open again. As he did, the door groaned and creaked. The hinges, although were free to move, complained of being made to do so. As Tony reopened the door once more, there was a loud cracking sound, the top hinge gave way and the door dropped and stopped swinging.

Michael pulled Tony away, afraid that the door was going to collapse on him. "what are you trying to do, you idiot. Are you trying to get yourself killed?".

Tony winced in pain. Michael had grabbed him a little too hard.

Tony turned to face us "this is getting messed up, that door wasn't like this earlier. Now look at it".

The door had suddenly now started to look its age. The base had gone through one of the floorboards, leaving a splintered gash in the floor.

Cobwebs connected the top to the ceiling. Varnish had peeled away from the large panels. It now looked like it had never moved at all earlier. Even though we had all witnessed its movement.

We turned and started to walk up the stairs to the upper landing. The light we had seen from outside was still on. The light from inside the attic room had cast its flickering light through the door in the room and onto the landing. The further across it travelled, the more faded it became. I had reached the top step first and I turned to face the room with the attic door inside. I could see the light dancing inside the room. The light was beaming across the bedroom floor. Michael and Tony arrived by my side. All three of us just stood amazed at what we were seeing. As we watched the floorshow, a shadow walked across the light, making us all jump.

I was the first to step back "what the hell was that?".

I hadn't realised that both Tony and Michael had jumped a couple of steps back.

With a quivering voice, Tony pointed towards the room "is that inside the room? Please say it's not".

Michael moved forward, "I don't think so, it looked like it was coming from the attic room. We need to find out, that could be Steve".

After a few moments, we gained our composure and cautiously walked into the room. From the moment we went back into the house, we felt that we were being watched. Tony could feel this and as we moved into the room, he kept peering behind us. "You can feel it too?" I asked.

"I'm sure we are being watched. The photos on the wall are really creeping me out. It's like in the horror movies, when the innocent victim is walking through the scary house and the eyes in the picture are moving with them. We have walked past three pictures and there are definitely no moving eyes, but it still feels like we are being watched". Tony replied.

"There is something in there and we must find out what it is, whether its Steve or not". Michael replied.

Without warning, the scream came again. The sound was the same as before. It echoed throughout the house. It came at us from all directions. The sound stopped and another could be heard. One at a time we could hear thuds coming from behind us.

"What the hell" I shouted above the sounds.

We all spun round to face the landing. From the far end, we could see the pictures that were clearly on the wall, were now sitting on the floor.

Some were broken. Then there was another thud on the floor.

Michael shone the torch down the landing, just as another picture had hit the floor and started to topple over.

Then another. This time we saw the picture fall. Another fell, then another. The time between each picture became less and less.

"oh shit, its coming towards us" Michael shouted.

Something was coming at us. Knocking the pictures off the wall as it got closer. Faster and faster it came. Until Michael couldn't take any more and lunged at the door. He slammed it shut, just as the last picture was knocked off the wall and hammered to the floor.

Then silence. Nothing.

Not even the wind from outside made any sound. I could see the branches through the window, swaying from side to side. But nothing came through, even though half the glass panels were missing.

After being rattled by the pictures coming off the wall, we just stood, looking at each other. The shock of the experience had gotten to us. We needed a moment to get our heads around what had just happened.

Finally, I snapped out of this strange moment.

"Steve. We must get Steve" I called out. Michael and Tony, both shook their heads.

"That was crazy "Michael remarked.

Tony agreed "This is too much. Let's just find Steve and get the hell out of here".

We turned to face the door that led up to the attic room.

The light was still flickering under the door.

Then we were slowly enveloped in darkness. The room went black apart from the small fragments of light in the remnants of the windows.

The light from under the doorway, dimmed and extinguished.

There was no sound, no clicking of a light switch. The light we saw had to of been either an open fire or a gas or oil lamp.

As we approached the door, an icy cold blast of air projected out from underneath and straight at us and although the wind hit me directly in the face, it sent a frozen chill throughout my body. We all felt it. After the wind subsided, we approached the door again. I leant forward to grip the door handle. This time I could feel searing heat emitting from it. Despite the cold wind that had barrelled through previously, the handle was hot. I rolled down my sleeve and wrapped it around my hand and grabbed the handle. Then we could smell smoke. The heat was that intense, that it was burning the sleeve, creating wisps of smoke to rise from my hand. I quickly pushed down on the handle and threw open the door. Tony took it upon himself and proceeded to walk into the doorway.

Then things turned really sour for us. As we looked into the dark void on the other side of the door, there was an almighty scream. It was so loud; we had to cup our hands around our ears. Suddenly and without warning, Tony was lifted off the floor by a couple of inches. He was suspended above the floor. Michael and I could see him struggling, as if something had hold of him and he was trying to break free from the grasp. His legs flailing back and forth. His arms waving around in front of him.

Then, his body tipped sideways, and his head slumped down.

With veracious speed, Tony's body came fly towards Michael and me.

With our arms outstretched, Tony's body hit us, knocking us to the floor on the far side of the room and away from the attic door.

We slumped to the floor, holding on to Tony. We were so confused by what had happened. We didn't see the shadow in the doorway watching us. With beady eyes it could see us writhing about on the floor in a tangled mess. It then turned, gripped the door panel and closed the door shut. As it did, the cold wind came back. It swirled around the room in a vortex and then slowly dispersed, leaving us dazed and confused on the floor.

After a moment Tony was the first to get up. "sod this I'm getting out now" he said and started to make his way out of the room.

Michael and I got up quick and chased after him. We rushed out onto the landing, kicking the fallen pictures as we did and shot down the stairs as fast as if our lives depended on it. We caught up with Tony at the bottom of the stairs. He was staring at the main door.

It was closed again, but how. It wasn't that long before, that the door was wide open, in tatters and hanging off its hinges.

Michael grabbed hold of the knob. "it's not opening, how can that be?".

I could hear intense fear in his voice. He was scared, although he was trying his best not to show it. "let me try, you wimp" and I gave it a tug. Like with Michael, the door wouldn't open. Now it was Tony's turn. He tugged and pulled at the door but as with Michael and I, the door wouldn't move.

There was a whoosh and a loud crashing sound, as an enormous vase came hurtling past our heads and smashed into the upper panels of the door, leaving splinters of porcelain hanging out of the slowly decaying wood. Plates of vase scattered about the floor amongst us.

"what the hell!". We turned and came face to face with what had thrown the vase.

Looking up to the top of the stairs, bold as brass, was the dark figure that had stood in the attic doorway earlier.

An eery sound started to fill the house, like an animal groaning with pain. Tony now lost all grip of reality "right, that's it. I don't care what that is up there. I will throw myself out the window before that thing gets me" he said, grabbing an old hat stand, positioned in the corner behind the door.

He took aim and launched the stand directly at the nearest window. To our amazement, instead of hearing the splintering sound of glass crashing to the floor. All we heard was a loud thudding noise and the stand came flying back at Tony. He dodged out of the way and it went skidding across the hallway floor and came to rest at the far end.

The groaning started to get louder. Just bearable, but louder just the same. "what is it doing up there? Is it going to just stand there or what?" Michael shouted. I thought he was trying to get its attention. Maybe he had had enough and was willing it to confront us. that wouldn't be my choice, but I wasn't going to stop him. I too, was getting angry at the situation.

I turned my head away from Michael and started to look up the staircase to where the entity was standing. I followed the crooked bannister to the top and to where it was standing. I could see a strange mist. It wasn't just any kind of mist; it was pale yellow in colour, but it had some sort of weight to it. It was oozed along the landing like a thick fluid. Yet it was transparent. As I stared transfixed, the mist started to clear, and I was able to see where it had come from.

The mist was oozing out from underneath what appeared to be thick curtain fabric. Intricate detail covered the outer edges with flowers and spiralling patterns. Then I noticed the figure within the fabric. once the mist had cleared a little more, I could make out that the figure was that of a tallish lady.

she was dressed in Victorian clothing. Her feet hidden from view by the mist. Then I concentrated on her features, her face was starting to take shape from the mist. I was shocked to see that it was a face of a reasonably young woman, possibly in her late twenties to early thirties. She was wearing a beautiful blue Victorian style dress that flowed around her ankles.

She had a perfectly rounded face. She was beautiful in every way. But looks could be deceiving, especially if she were the one responsible for Steve going missing. Her dark blonde hair was neatly tied back into a tight bun.

Then the groaning noise ceased, and she began to speak. A soft but demanding, concerned voice came down from the landing to us.

"You do not belong here. Leave now or you will never leave. If my husband catches you, I don't know what he'll do".

Michael wasn't taking any nonsense and shouted back at her "who the hell are you?".

For a moment, there was no reply, eventually there was a quiet reply.

"my name is of no concern to you; I need you to leave and quickly".

I looked up at her again, only now, I was starting to see the wall behind her. She was starting to disappear as she started to step back.

I pointed to the far end of the landing "we are not leaving without our friend; he was in that room and now he has gone. We want to know where he is, so we can go".

By the time I had finished talking, she was barely a silhouette against the wall "he won't be coming back".

Tony raced to the bottom of the stairs "what have you done with our friend you bitch!".

I thought he was going to run up the stairs and throttle the nearly invisible woman. But he just stood there shaking his clenched fist at her.

Whilst I was busy looking at tony, the woman had no form anymore, she had reverted back to the mist we first saw.

"where is our friend please? You must tell us" I called out. It seemed strange talking to flaking wallpaper on the wall, but something told me that she could still hear everything we were saying.

Then faintly, her voice came from halfway down the stairs. "my husband took him, and he will do the same to you, if you don't leave. Please I beg of you, he will kill you, if he catches you".

With that, the mist cleared, and all had gone silent. She had made her warning.

Tony spun round and looked directly at me. "what the hell does she mean? Did she say that Steve was dead and if we stick around, he will do the same to us too?".

"it would seem that way" I relied.

He then turned back to the stairs "well, I think he'd better come and get us then, because we are not leaving without him". I was shocked. We rarely saw this side of Tony. I was just about to calm him down when Michael saved me the trouble. Suddenly there was a loud thud as he hit the floor and scaring the living daylights out of us.

I rushed over to him and knelt by his side, "are you ok mate?" I whispered to him.

"yeah, I think so, did you see that, after Tony shouted at her?" he replied.

"see what?"

He slowly raised his hand.

"look there on the wall. Right next to where she was standing. There is a picture there. All the pictures had fallen off the wall earlier. That one was definitely not there".

With hearing that, Tony rushed up the stairs, grabbed the picture and with as much sure footedness as he could muster, came running back down again. Missing some of the steps as he did until he was standing back in front of me and Michael.

He thrust the picture out into the middle of us.

"here it is, look at it". And he held it higher, so we could get a clearer look.

A shiver shot down my spine. It was the woman we had seen on the stairs. She was standing at the front of the house, with a small child playing in front of her. He was playing with a wooden spinning top.

The picture was hand painted with quite a lot of detail. The main thing that got me, was that it looked like it had only been painted the day before. "why isn't the husband in the picture?" Michael asked.

"I don't know. Maybe he was the one who painted it". I replied turning my eyes to the bottom right corner. In dark lettering was the name B. AMBERSEAL.

Michael by now had gained his composure and was slowly picking himself up off the floor.

"Right! We got the warning. Let's just get Steve and go" he said.

"maybe at the same time, we could find out, who these people were". I said and put the picture down, leaning it up against the door frame.

"are you nuts" Tony shouted "just get Steve and go. We are not here for a history trip. We just want out of this shithole, right?".

Michael agreed. I felt that Tony was right, but I wanted to know.

The house was really starting to get to us, but we had to press on.

We walked up the stairs and made our way down the landing to the room where Steve had vanished. As we entered the room, we could still see clearly, the patch of blood on the ceiling and the floor. But it looked different. The blood wasn't congealing. It was still very fluid in movement and still very red.

After staring directly at the patch on the floor for a moment and focusing my eyes on the centre of the puddle, I blinked. Then I blinked again in disbelief. Droplets of blood were dripping from the blood on the floor and going up to the patch on the ceiling. It was as if the house was upside down, or we were.

"oh shit "Tony shouted.

"what's the matter?"

"I think I have just stood in something nasty"

Michel chuckled "what, like dog shit?".

"What is dog shit doing up here? Shouldn't it be outside?".

Tony lifted up his foot and started looking at the sole of his shoe "somehow I don't think its dog shit, but far worse than that".

Something red and sticky was clinging to his foot. Tendrils were hanging in places dripping blood onto the floor. I followed the droplets of blood and they slowly moved towards the large patch of blood on the floor. Here and there on his sole, were odd darkish lumps. They too were moving, I thought that it was due to gravity until one such lump, started moving sideways.

I pushed Tony away from the puddle. he stumbled.

"why the hell did you do that?" he called out.

"wipe your foot quickly "I replied.

The he noticed it too and started rubbing his foot along the floor and scraping at the walls, removing the stuff off his foot.

Michael ran into the opposite corner and proceeded to be sick, spraying bile and remnants of his lunch onto the walls and floor.

Tony joined me at my side. "great this is all we need. One person missing, one blowing chunks in the corner, this is going to end great isn't it?".

"To be honest I wasn't feeling great myself" I replied.

We heard Michael gargle, then spit on the floor "I'm good" he said and came back to the centre of the room.

We stood there staring at the blood. We all agreed that it was like the house was upside down, it was as if there was something bleeding under the floorboards. The blood was oozing out and dripping upwards into the ceiling and through into the attic. Both patches weren't getting any bigger, but then, they weren't getting any smaller either.

We stood and carried on watching the blood dripping upwards. More and more droplets dripped into patch above us. "somethings definitely playing with us" I mumbled to myself.

Michael must of heard me, I didn't realise I was talking aloud "your right but is this Steve's blood?" he said.

I started picking under my fingernails, which was something I did when I was nervous " I hope not, but I have a sneaky feeling that we are going to have to go up into the loft to find out" I replied.

Tony shook his head "I am not going up there, no way ".

Michael let out a smirk "that's about right. One sign of trouble and you turn your back and run".

"no, it's not. You can see it with your own two eyes. You've heard it with your own ears, we all did. If we stay here any longer, we will end up the same as Steve. Tony replied.

Michael had a habit of winding Tony up, just to provoke a reaction. We had told Tony many times to ignore him, but Michael always knew what to say and how to say it.

"do you fancy going up there then Michael?"

"No, I don't, and you certainly aren't going to make me" Michael snapped back, showing his annoyance.

I stepped in "right! So, what do you suggest we do then? If Steve is up there, I'm sure he would appreciate it, if we helped to get him out".

Both Tony and Michaels heads bowed down. I was annoyed at the pair of them. With Steve missing, the last thing we could do, was start bickering amongst ourselves and now they realised it.

"sort it out, you two. This is getting nothing done and we are no closer to finding Steve" I shouted in anger

I looked around on the floor for a piece of wood or something to poke around with. Fairly close by was what appeared to be a piece of picture frame. It must have come from one of the pictures outside the room on the landing and bounced into this room after hitting the floor.it certainly would do the job.

I picked up the wood and moved towards the puddle on the floor and went to poke it. Then it moved. It was as if it knew what I was going to do. As the stick approached it, the blood moved out of the way and disappeared under the floorboards.

"quick, lift up the boards and get to it from there, it couldn't have gone that quickly "Michael said nervously.

"I'm not taking anything up, if that woman was right and I'm hoping she's not, then I'm opting out of making the situation worse, by ripping up her house. Let's just look at the one on the ceiling".

In agreement, I stood up and reached up. Before I could get to it, it was gone. All that remained, was a tired looking ceiling.

As I brought my arm down, not wanting to believe what I had been seeing, there was an almighty shout from the other end of the landing and the sound of a door slamming shut. The sound was horrifying. It wasn't the same as before. This time it was the sound of a man's voice and he wasn't happy.

Tony looked straight at me with angry eyes "that's it, now I'm really pissed off with all of this" he shouts, and he stormed out of the room and onto the landing and then he was gone.

By the time I got to the doorway and peered down across the gloomily lit landing, Tony had vanished into thin air.

Now Michael and I were on our own. There had been no noise, no shout from Tony, nothing.

Michael joined me on the landing, "what now? We have two people missing and no idea where they are".

I grabbed Michaels sleeve and tried to drag him down the stairs, but he was stuck fast where he stood, he didn't want to go.

"we have got to think of something, we can't just leave them here".

"Don't you think I don't know that. I've also had enough of this shit and you're right, we can't just leave them here. There is a mobile phone in the car. We get back to the car, ring the police and wait for them to arrive and deal with it". I replied.

Michaels eyebrows pointed down in the middle in anger. "why didn't that get mentioned when Steve went missing?".

All I could do was shrug my shoulders.

"we could have called them then and we wouldn't have to be going through all this shit!".

It was now my turn to get angry, "yeah, well I didn't think of it then, but I have thought of it now, so let that be the end of it. Let's just get out of here and get that mobile. The longer you and I stand here arguing the toss, the more likely we are at never getting out of here".

Finally, Michael started to move, and we made our way down to the front door. I grabbed the door handle and turned. The door was locked.

"ok sherlock, what now?" Michael remarked.

"we will have to find an alternative way out, it's not that difficult. If you remember, there was a door round the back, where that goo was oozing out of the door".

Michael understood but he started shaking his head. "doesn't that mean that we have to go through parts of the house that we haven't explored?".

I could tell Michael was scared stiff. I was too. But I had to put my fear to one side for our own sakes. "we have no other choice, if it means getting out of here, then I will be glad to go whatever way we have too" and I pushed him towards a door to the side of the staircase.

As I did, Michael pirouetted on his heals and made a quick side-step. This made me lunge forward into the door.

Michael pointed at the door. "I'm not going in there first, if your so brave, then you go in and I will follow". I was impressed with his move, but also quite unimpressed as to why he did it.

"does it really matter? We both need to get out!" I replied.

"ok, I will go first, but get ready to run, if we have too".

I looked down at the doorknob. There was no slime in sight, so I took hold of it and started to turn.

It felt warm to the touch, as if someone had been living in the next room and had had a fire going at some point. I felt no fear as I gently opened the door. As soon as the door started to clear the frame, I could see light from inside. I turned my head to look at Michael, he was right behind me. I motioned my finger to my mouth "shh, I think there is someone in here". Michaels eyes suddenly flew wide open in shock.

I pushed the door a little more. Inside the room, was a similar dull light, that we saw before upstairs. The atmosphere felt different. It felt inviting and comfortable.

It was a Victorian kitchen. Immaculate in every way. It didn't look anything like the rest of the house at all. Copper pans hung from a wooden chandelier in the middle of the kitchen. This hung over a central workbench. They were so clean and untarnished. They had to of taken a long time to clean.

To the far side of the kitchen, were a couple of porcelain basins. They too were spotless. Neither of them showed any age at all.

I noticed, that around the tops of the walls, were an abundance of horseshoes and strap buckles from horses bridalwear.

While looking at this amazing sight, I had failed to notice what was laying in the central table. Michael tapped me on the shoulder and a pointed hand reached past my head.

Then I saw it. A comparative feast was placed there, by whom was another issue for my mind to get around. A large roast foul was the centrepiece, I had never seen a turkey that big before. Surrounding it on the silver tray, were various vegetables. In large bowls were more vegetables.

I was never a fan of vegetables, but the way I was feeling at that moment, I would have eaten anything that was put in front of me.

Scattered around the outer edges of the table, were different desserts, cakes and biscuits. Scattered about the table, here and there, were copper jugs full of fluid. I peered inside one and inhaled the fragrance coming from within. It smelt very floral and sweet.

Michael approached the table and started to tuck into the food.

"what the hell are you doing? are you mad? "I shouted.

Michael suddenly dropped the food and lifted his guilt-ridden face.

"what's the problem?" he replied.

"you really think that, in a deserted house like this, someone is going to keep only this room in spotless condition, kill two of our friends and then cook us a bloody feast? C'mon, listen to reason" I replied.

Michael dropped a roast potato onto the table as I pulled him away.

"I suppose so".

Tempting though it was, to sit down and cram as much food into my face as I could, there was still doubt in my mind. That lady had warned us, and I was worried that her husband was setting us up.

"what if this is him?" I asked.

"oh my god. Your right. He could have done this".

We managed to resist temptation. The food was enticing but we were able to resist and started to walk towards the back door.

There was no sign of goo by the back door either. Although we clearly saw there was on the other side when we were outside it earlier.

So, it was a case of hoping that this door was locked, like the main front door.

I reached for the handle, it too felt warm. There was a click as the handle turned. The door started to pull too, when there was a faint voice from the far side of the kitchen.

"please don't leave us here" and the door closed by itself.

Michael barged passed me to get to the door. "get out of my way, I'm not staying here anymore and listening to that crap!" he said and tried to reopen the door. But the door stood fast and wouldn't open.

He eventually gave up and frowned as he walked over and propped himself up against the basins.

I turned to face the far end of the kitchen and almost jumped out of the window. Standing in front of the door that lead out to the stairway, was the woman.

The pale-yellow mist, still flowing out from under her dress and creeping around the bottom of the table.

Her mouth slowly opened and the softest of words could be heard. "please don't leave us here, he will get us. he already has your friends".

"your husband?" I asked.

Michael stepped in "we can't help you if you don't start giving us some answers".

A fading voice returned. "yes, my husband. He wants all of you".

As I looked back, she had gone again and all that remained of her was a wisp of yellow mist and the pale light of the kitchen. All the food had gone, and everything started to age. The shiny copper pans tarnished fast, going from their shiny orange, to a dark brown. The two basins cracked and changed from pure white, to a dark cream and green stains started to appear on the sides.

Then the back door opened by itself and we took the opportunity to walk out of the house. As we walked, I turned to face the back of the house and noticed the door had closed and the light had gone from the kitchen. We were in the darkness again.

Within seconds, we were running back to the car.

"now, let's phone the police and get this sorted" Michael wheezed.

I opened the driver's door and grabbed the mobile phone off the dashboard as I sat down.

I unlocked the phone and dialled the number ask quickly as I could, not knowing what was going to happen next.

If I did, I probably wouldn't have bothered picking up the phone in the first place.

Chapter three

The phone rang twice, then I heard a strange tone. Briefly there were faint whispers on the other end, then a click. The phone went dead. I looked at the darkened screen, swiped my finger to switch it on. Still nothing. The phone was completely dead.

I placed the phone down and looked at Michael.

"what's happened? Did anyone answer?".

"no, just some strange whispering and then it hung up. Now the phone has gone completely. The battery is totally dead. The weird thing is, I have heard the whispering before".

"that can't be, I was on the phone when we first arrived here, there had to of been at least sixty percent on there". He replied, walking up to the car and taking the phone.

'help yourself' I thought.

He started pressing the buttons and the screen. It wouldn't switch on.

"bloody start, you, stupid phone" he shouted at it and threw it to the floor. As it hit the ground, the phone burst into life. The screen shone with bright white blinding light. Then a face appeared briefly. The phone emitted a loud scream, then went black again.

Michael lifted his foot "heap of shit" and started to bring it down onto the phone. I jumped in and swiped it from underneath him before he could take our only way out of the place away from us.

As I held the phone in my hand, wondering how that face appeared on the phone. It lit up again. This time it didn't scream, and the face didn't appear. It was just pure white, but the whispering had returned.

I held the phone up to my ear and tried to listen over Michaels ranting.

From the earpiece, I could clearly hear a voice coming through. It started quietly and got louder with each passing second, as if it were walking towards me.

Michael had gone quiet. He had seen me holding the phone to the side of my head.

I looked at him. "there's someone on the other end ".

Again, the voice spoke. It was the woman from the kitchen. He voice was soft and unmistakeable.

"please, you cannot go. You must stay and help me and my son". Between some words, I could hear faint sniffles, as if someone had been crying.

"what can we do? You're not even here". I replied, still trying to make sense of the whole situation.

The voice became clearer still and the sobbing sounds had stopped. "I am here and all around you. You are the first people that have been here in sixty years".

"what happened to the others that came here then?". I didn't want to sound stupid or obvious. Which I was clearly doing because of our present set of circumstances.

"I took the wrong approach and confronted them before anything could go wrong. As a result, they fled". She replied.

"so, you decided to allow your husband to kill one of my friends, before you made contact with us? now I have lost another friend and we are no closer to getting out of here".

I was annoyed and angry with her and I was starting to lose control of my emotions.

"ok, so you need our help. What are we supposed to do? We are not ghost hunters".

"go to the southern end of the garden, you will find some answers there". 'strange answer' I thought. But felt that we hadn't really got much of a choice.

Just as I was going to ask what we were to be looking for, her voice started to get louder. It began to change, and the voice of a man started to growl.

"leave my wife alone! Or when I find you, your fate will be the same as your friends".

My anger took control "sorry matey, but we are not leaving without them. If we don't get our friends back, then I guess, we will be staying the night".

"what!" Michael shouted. "are you out of your fucking mind?".

"then you will have to die and join your friends here in the house".

He had the sound of authority, but I was well prepared to go against that, in order to retrieve my friends. Michael also got angry with him. "we're sorry arsehole, but we are staying right here until we get our friends back and if it means talking to that very charming young lady, you call your wife. Then so be it".

I could tell Michael was now wound up like a coiled spring and any minute he would explode with energy. He held up a fist to thin air, pointing it towards the house and taking a step forward. I was about to try and calm him down, but it was too late. He went over the edge.

"what she saw in you in the first place, I don't know. If that's what we have to do to get out of here, then sod you we are going to help her".

It was a bold statement, but it had to be said.

Then, without warning the phone screen brightened, I could hear a whistle, then it burst into flames, making me drop it to the floor.

We could hear it making a fizzing noise, as flames burst out the sides. Then we could hear something else, a man's laughter, it was deep, and it was coming from the phone.

The laughter started to fade and became more of a gargle and as it did, the phone started to melt. The flames stopped. All that was left was a bubbling mess on the floor. Every time the bubbles popped; I could swear that I could still hear the contorted laughter. Until there was nothing. Just a messy pile of plastic on the ground.

Michael poked my shoulder "what are we going to do now then?".

"I guess we are going to have to go down to the bottom of the garden and see what the lady was going on about" I replied.

"you're shitting me, right?".

"no, I'm not. If we are going to find out what's happed to Steve and Tony, then we are going to have to do what the woman asked. If it means going down there, then we have to. It may be the only answer".

"you're mad, you are. Fucking mad. I'm not going down there, even if that is what she wants you to do. It could be a trap. We could get down there and something could happen to one or both of us. either way, I'm not going" he snapped back at me.

I took hold of him and gave him an aggressive shake. "what is wrong with you? You never used to be like this, for fuck sake. You never used to be scared of anything. Now look at you, you're cowering away. We've been through too much to turn tails and run away. Plus, what's Sarah going to say, when she finds out? Are you going to tell her what happened? ".

Michael just stood there, shaking his head.

"exactly, I didn't think you would, now stop being an idiot and let's get on with this, we haven't got that far to go".

I was pleasantly surprised. Michael all of a sudden, lifted his head and puffed himself up, expanding his chest as he did.

"you're right, what am I like. I never used to be like this. Let's do this!" he replied.

I rubbed his shoulder, "good, let's go" and we walked towards the back garden.

"what do you think we will find down there?" Michael asked.

"I don't know, but if it brings Steve and Tony back, I'm not bothered".

"good, I'm up for it. Let's go".

We walked round the side of the house and towards the back door of the kitchen. To our right were small steppingstones which led off into the darkness of the garden. I turned on the torch to light up the overgrown garden.

"that woman isn't expecting us to go down there, is she?".

"of course, that's where she told us to go. To the bottom of the garden".

I knew that Michael was still a little bit worried about all of this, so I took the opportunity and started to take slow steps onto the stones. Michael followed with caution.

I turned to look at Michael "just keep your eyes open and lookout for anything unusual. I have a funny feeling that he won't bother us down there, otherwise she wouldn't direct us out here.

"are you sure she isn't setting us up?" he replied.

"I don't think so. Every time she appeared, she seemed to be scared of her husband. If she were going to harm us, she would have done so by now" "we still need to be careful" I pleaded.

"right. If it's a trap, we get out fast. Find a police station and tell them what is happening here". I followed with reassuringly.

After a few more steps, the darkness of the night had completely set in. I could only just see the stones without the light of the torch.

We had already walked about seven stones; I could just make out where the rest of them were. There were about twenty in total leading they're way down the garden. After a few more steps, a pure white light shone down on Michael and me. I looked up. Just above the house, the moon was peering out from behind the clouds and clearing the tops of the trees, casting an illuminous shade on everything we could see.

The garden itself look beautiful at night. The grass wasn't too overgrown. You could still see the stones clearly, even though the house had not been lived in for over a century. Around the edges of the garden, lay small bushes, with pale coloured flowers glistening in the moonlight. Every part of the garden had areas where plants grew.

To the far end of the garden, we could clearly see, overgrown trees and shrubs. This area was strange, as it did not go with the rest of the property. This was obviously not respected as well as the rest of the garden.

Michael and I continued to follow the stones which led us to the area.

"do you think that's where she wants us to go?" Michael asked.

"I reckon, there isn't really anywhere else we could go. There aren't any other paths. So, it looks like that's where we are heading" I replied.

I placed my hands into the thick foliage at the edge of the lawn and parted the branches of an ancient willow tree and was shocked at what I saw in the clearing on the other side.

I stood there with Michael peering over my shoulder. Inside the dome of the willow tree, were completely clear of vegetation. No grass grew. Instead, what lay there, were fine piles of wood chips and bark.

From somewhere, a pleasant smell, wafted through the branches. We couldn't smell it before we entered the willow. I could only describe the smell as to that of potpourri. This part of the garden had a calm feeling. Exactly the same as that of the kitchen. It was warm, the chill of the night had not entered this area at all.

Michael pushed me in the back "look over there by the base of the tree".

I turned to the side and looked directly at the trunk of the willow.

There, propped up in front of the tree, were two partly decayed gravestones. The largest of the two, was a patterned cross, with an angel standing behind it, with its wings unfurled. Next to it, was a much smaller gravestone. A simple half circle stone with writing etched into it.

I walked closer so I could read the inscriptions, which, even with the cover of the branches, I was able to see.

On the large stone were the words 'HERE LIES JAY, DIED 1/11/1827'. There was nothing else written.

"look at this stone Mike. There is no 'IN LOVING MEMORY OF' on there".

Michael stepped over and shone the torch onto the gravestones.

"The smaller one looks worse, look" he said, pointing at the graves.

At a glance there was nothing there, then after I focused a little, it only had one word written. The name 'TOBY' in scruffy lettering appeared. This was not a carved headstone; this had been scratched onto it.

What wasn't making sense, was that great care had been taken on the large stone, yet the smaller stone, had no care or attention made to it at all. it was as if no one cared for the person that lay buried beneath it and only a reminder, that at one time there was a life on this property.

Michael stood looking at the two gravestones with a strange glance. "why do you think the tall one has all the markings on it and yet just a name on the small one?" he asked.

I got up off my knees and faced Michael. Before I could say anything, a bright yellow light came through the willow branches and the two stones were illuminated in light.

"what the fuck is that Wayne?" Michael shouted at the top of his voice. I could hear fear in every word he spoke. It made me spin round to face the stones. The light itself stopped in front of the gravestones. It was very similar to the light we had seen twice inside the house. The light was just floating there. Then it started swaying from side to side. Then something changed.

The light started emitting heat. It was getting warmer and warmer.

It got so hot that we had to take a couple of steps backwards in case we got burned. Then it started to change shape. It became a horizontal shape.

"I think we need to get out of here!" Michael pleaded.

"no! please don't go!" said a soft voice from inside the light.

It was the woman again. Michael started to walk away. "you're Michael, aren't you? "the voice asked.

With that, Michael stopped dead in his tracks. Paused for a moment, then turned around. "how do you know who I am?".

"I don't know much, but I know that you two must help me. I was able to speak to one of your friends, the one you call Steve".

"you spoke with Steve?" I asked.

"yes. He told me about how you all ended up here. Unfortunately, my husband took him away before I could free him".

Michael bowed his head "so Steve is dead then?".

"I'm sorry, but yes he is. He has been trying to communicate with you, but like everyone in our realm, it takes a while to be able to appear to the living" she replied.

"you mean, like a ghost?" Michael asked as he walked back by my side.

"yes. If he can get away from my husband's grasp, he may get the energy and the knowhow to get in contact with you".

I was uncomfortable, talking to a floating lightbulb. I looked at Michael, then looked back at the light. "I'm sorry, but if we are going to have this conversation, then we are going to have to do it face to face", I said. At the same time, I was thinking that, I had put the final nail in the coffin and sealed our fate. But surprisingly the light got brighter. Michael and I had to shield our eyes. then the light started to fade, we brought our hands down. I could see the woman from before, standing in front of us.

She was looking sad; I wasn't sure how or why. I looked directly into her eyes and felt some sort of gravitational pull, reaching out to me, taking hold and pulling me towards her.

She raised her right hand and wiped away a couple of tears from her cheek. I noticed how smooth and pure; her skin looked. Not a blemish in sight.

Then I got a big surprise.

She smiled. Showing, perfect and level teeth. "is this better for you?" she asked.

"that's better" I replied.

"so, who are you and what is it that we can do to help you?" Michael asked.

I thought it was quite rude to just simply jump in and ask flat out right. But time was of the essence.

"My name is Jay".

I quickly butted in. "your lady Jay".

"yes" she replied.

"how? The woman in the picture looked really old and you are clearly not".

"yes, I know, that picture is how I would have looked, if it wasn't for him" she replied.

I was a little confused. "what do you mean by that?" I asked her.

"lives are mapped out and mine was cut short, so the picture shows me at an old age, in fact, my life was due to end three weeks after that was done". She explained.

"your husband killed you, but why?".

Jay let out a little sigh "he found out, the child we had, was not his".

"and that would be the gravestone that lies next to yours?" and Michael shone the torch down to the child's gravestone.

"that's right. I have been waiting for a long time for someone to come and help me stop him. But every time I try, people get hurt".

I paused for a moment, took a deep breath and prayed that the words I spoke next wouldn't return to haunt me.

"we will help you, if you can help us" I replied.

Lady Jay then turned to Michael "I need to say a few things to Wayne if you don't mind".

I was shocked. Why couldn't she just say what she needed to say in front of him. Then I found out.

Michael walked outside the protection of the willow branches and waited.

Lady Jay placed her hands together. "I'm sorry for that, but what I have to say is only for you to hear. I'm afraid he is not going to make it away from here. He will join Steve".

"what about Tony? Is he dead?" I asked.

"as far as I can tell, he is still alive. But for how long, I don't know".

"so, where is he?".

"I'm not sure. He is still inside the house somewhere and you will see him again".

"are we going to get away from here?" I pleaded.

"yes. You will". She replied.

I stood there thinking. 'just perfect. What a great weekend. We stumble across this house and it's the last place we are ever going to see'.

She took a step closer to me. "you will leave here and lead a good life".

"how do you know that?" I asked.

She reached out her arms and warm hands took hold of mine.

"in the near future, you will find someone special as I did".

I felt like I was about to laugh and managed to stop myself.

"what like your ex-husband?" I chuckled.

"no. I found someone, who was much kinder. Someone who cared for me more than he ever could". Then there was an awkward silence.

"that person was you!". She finally revealed.

That freaked me out. I could feel my legs going numb and they started to wobble. I took hold of the trunk of the willow, to stop myself from collapsing onto the floor. My breathing started to become laboured. I didn't understand what she had just told me.

"what do you mean, that person was me? I'm me". Somehow, she must see me as someone she knew when she was alive.

"my husband and I were married for three years, until he found out that the child, I bore wasn't his. He didn't take it well at first. Then he went berserk".

"he found out that your child wasn't his, so he killed you?" I asked.

"yes. He went mad, saying that I was only meant for him and nobody else. He killed Toby in front of me, to show his disgust".

"couldn't you stop him?".

"I couldn't. he knew I would fight to save Toby. So, he waited for the right opportunity and threw me down the staircase. Then he tied a rope around his neck and made me watch".

"then what?". Things were starting to become clearer, but I wanted to know everything. If our lives were in danger, then we had to know what we were dealing with. Especially about her husband and what he was like.

"This is taking too long to explain, I will show you what happened". She placed her hands on my temples and things started to become blurred.

There was a jolt of energy and everything went dark. The darkness didn't last. Within seconds, the scene changed. My vision started to brighten, and a new image replaced the view of the willow tree and the gravestones. I was back inside the house, standing just inside the front door. Everything looked new and clean. The wallpaper looked fresh. There was no dirt or dust anywhere. Lady Jay had taken me back to her time.

As I looked around at the sight before me, I could hear shouting coming from one of the bedrooms. All of a sudden, one of the bedroom doors on the right of the landing, flew open and Lady Jay came flying out at some speed and landed in a heap on the floor in the middle of the landing.

"you won't be doing that again!" came a voice from within the bedroom. Then he was standing in the doorway, looking down at her, he had a hold of Toby. I took a small leap towards the bottom of the stairs and came to an abrupt stop in mid motion. Something was stopping me from getting any closer. There was an unseen force trying to push me back.

"don't you touch her!" I shouted.

The demand had fallen on deaf ears. He didn't hear a word I said and continued to pace towards Jay, Toby being dragged along behind him. He leaned over and grabbed her by the arm and lifted her off the floor. Struggling, her husband dragged them both to the top of the stairs. Without care, he pushed threw her over the edge of the stairs and in slow motion, I watched her as she fell down. Her body twisting and turning in all manner of impossible directions. I could hear bones cracking and breaking as she came down. Then she came to a contorted stop at the bottom. She had a small cut just behind her left temple, but it wasn't bleeding too much. I was desperate to help, but I was unable to move.

Toby was next. He was thrown into the air and fortunately, Toby managed to find his balance and landed on his feet. He just stood there shocked at what was happening. He stood there motionless, just long enough to see his mother coming round from the fall. He was glad his mother was still alive. But for how long was another question.

Jay knew her son was looking at her and slowly turned her head to face him. They both smiled at each other, until Jay saw something that turned her face from sympathy to fear. Standing a few feet behind Toby, was Jay's husband. He was furious. He was going to throw him down the stairs to join his mother, but Toby ruined his plan. He disappeared into one of the rooms and returned with a length of what looked like rope and was now quietly creeping up behind Toby.

The last thing she saw, before she temporarily lost her vision, was her husband grabbing hold of poor Toby's arm. She turned her head away, to face a small pool of blood. She didn't want to see anymore. She knew what was going to happen to her son.

I also knew what was about to happen and no matter how hard I tried; I could not turn away.

The crazy man was dragging the poor boy along the landing. He got about halfway along, then stopped. I could now see that what looked like rope, was actually a long curtain cord. Violet in colour with yellow threads running through it. Instead of tying back the curtains, it was going to now be used for a more sickening task. He started to wrap the cord around Toby's neck. Toby was pleading with him not too. But the evil man, clearly wouldn't listen.

"please don't kill me!" Toby pleaded.

Jay had started sobbing "please don't do this".

There was an evil look in his eyes. One that showed no remorse.

48.

He was going to kill him, whether he had to listen to the begging or not. He was determined that there was going to be a death in the house that night.

Toby's face was starting to turn red. His airways being restricted by the cord. He was no longer pleading with him to stop. All I could hear was a faint rattle as he was gasping for air. With the cord in place, he picked Toby up and held him up towards the ceiling. Looking at jay he started shouting again.

"this is an abomination! You have disgraced my family and so, you and your devil spawn will die!".

Both Jay and Toby where crying. I was hurting for them. The scene that was playing out before me was too much and I didn't want to see anymore, so I closed my eyes. They just merely blinked. As my eyes opened again, I saw Toby's body floating in mid-air, as he was hurled over the edge of the landing bannister. His body started to drop like a stone, racing towards the ground.

I could see the cord tightening as he got closer the ground and prepared myself for what I was going to see next.

Within seconds, the cord snapped back on his body. Toby's legs flipped up into the air and he began to bounce and writhe in agony as his life was ebbing away. Arms and legs flailing in all directions as the cord started cutting deep into his throat and breaking just about every bone in Toby's fragile neck. Blood started to trickle out of his neck, over the chord and down to his now lifeless body and drip from his feet to the highly varnished floor.

Jay screamed "no!".

Toby stopped moving. His body, now, just dangled like a maggot on a fishing line. His limbs down by his side and completely motionless. The only movement was his entire body swinging by the chord.

I could hear his body banging against the wall with a sickening thud. It didn't seem real. It was like watching a horror movie.

All this time, Jays husband just stood there laughing. Now he had to finish what he started.

Jay was still crying on the floor, where she landed, after he threw her down the stairs. He looked at Toby, then turned his gaze at Jay "I'm sorry, but that's what happens, when you betray me".

"you bastard" she yelled back.

This made him laugh even more. I was furious, not just at him for what he was doing, but also with myself, because I was powerless to stop him. But now I understood why I was seeing this and why we were at the house. He had to be stopped, it was just a case of how.

"now, now, now, your turn is coming". With that, he started slowly walking down the stairs towards Jay.

"come now. Let's go and see your precious Toby, shall we" he yelled and grabbed her arm. As he lifted her, she tried to gain her footing, but at some point, as she was falling down the stairs, she must have damaged her ankle and she slumped back down to the floor. It wasn't going to stop him though. He simply dragged her along the floor and into the fairly large pool of blood beneath Toby's body.

"well, aren't you going to say goodbye to your precious son?".

"no. don't do this!" she begged.

He placed his arms under hers and lifted her up off the floor. He held her up in front of Toby's body.

Jay had gained some balance and stood there sobbing for her son.

"you will say goodbye to him!" and with deliberate movement, he rammed her head into Tobies completely lifeless body.

I couldn't take anymore, and I stood there begging to be out of this nightmare she had brought me too.

My prayers were answered just in time. He pulled her face away from Toby's body. She was covered in his blood. Just as the vision started to fade, I saw him pull out an old fishing knife and held it to her throat.

The last thing I saw before everything went black, was him drawing the knife across her neck, opening her throat. All I could hear, was his laughter and the gargling sound of the blood bubbling in Jay's throat as she gasped for breath.

Chapter four

Then I was back in front of Jay and Toby's graves, in front of the willow tree.

Jays hands were still on my temples. "he did that to you?" I asked.

She brought her hands down to her sides, "yes, and he won't allow us to rest".

"so, what have I got to do with all of this?" I asked.

She gave me a smile "when this is all over, providing you succeed. We will meet again and soon". She replied.

I was confused by this, but at this precise moment in time, I was more interested in finding my friends and going home.

"what do you want us to do then?" Michael asked walking back towards us.

She faced Michael. "his grave is over there at the holly bush".

Michael then butted in. "we haven't got to dig him up have we? I'm not digging nothing up".

"I'm sorry, but you will need too. When he was buried. He had some things in his possession, that has kept us bound to this torment".

"Like what?" I asked.

"he has items from Toby and me in his pockets. They must be taken away from him, then we should be free from his grasp".

Michael sneered "so now we are grave robbers. Great!".

I looked at him "it seems to be the only way. We have got to do this if we want to get out of here. You know she is right".

"but do you think she is telling the truth?" he asked.

After what I had seen, there was no doubt that she needed the help. It was now a case of persuading Michael that it's the best thing to do.

"yes. She is telling the truth and I intend on doing something about it. If not for Jay and Toby, then for Steve and Tony, and I will do it without you if I have too". I was getting annoyed with Michael. His cowardice was starting to return.

"so, you will help us Wayne?".

I turned back to Jay "we don't have much of a choice, but yes we will help".

"thank you, I will help as much as I possibly can" she replied and with that, her image started to change back into the ball of light. It started to dance in front of her gravestone, then dropped into the ground.

"we must be mad" Michael laughed.

"yes, we are, but what real choice do we have. Steve's gone, Tony's missing. If we are next, we may as well die trying to get something out of all this crap!" I snapped back. But would Michael accept the fact that we might not come out of this alive.

He patted me on the back "let's go and kick some spectral butt then" and with a funny sort of pigeon step, he made his way out from under the willow tree.

The holly bush was easy to spot, its branches had been left to grow. Without being cut back it was allowed to grow at a ferocious rate.

In the dark, it looked similar to the willow tree, only darker. It also took the dome like appearance. The spikey leaves becoming visible the closer we got. My nerves were in tatters, but still we pushed on.

We stood in front of the holly. The branches and foliage were thick. On looking, we couldn't see any obvious signs of a grave and I started to walk around the other side and there it was. The madman's grave.

It was a small stone, roughly the same size as Toby's. on it were the words 'IN MEMORY OF GEOFF'.

I almost lost it when Michael appeared behind me. "so, Geoff is the arseholes name then?" he whispered.

I knelt down and took a closer look. The carving at the top of the stone, looked like the back of the house. "come see this Mike" I called. He knelt down beside me. "it's the house". "look at the area of the attic" and pointed to the top of the stone. In the small effigy of the attic window, someone had carved a skull and crossbones. I wondered if there was some bizarre link to the light being on in that room, it all seemed a little too coincidental.

Michael looked around the back "there is a poem round here, look!". He called.

I peered round, and carved in deep letters and clearly visible, was a short poem. It read

A LIFE HAS BEEN TAKEN,

AND SHOULD NOT BE FORGOT.

REVENGE IS FOR THE LIVING,

FOR THE DEAD IT IS NOT.

'A strange poem' I thought, but a good one none the less. I had never heard that one before.

I looked at Michael "what do you think of that then mate?" I asked.

He just looked at me with a shocked look. "it's weird, but it's a good one. You should write it down". He replied.

"don't be daft, its off a grave, have some respect, regardless of who's grave it is".

"after what he did, don't you think he deserves it?".

I got up and to our surprise, Jay was standing behind us. we hadn't seen the light, that we normally see when she appears. It made both of us jump. "where did you come from? You could have scared us to death".

"the poem was put there by my father".

"why?" Michael asked, picking himself up off the floor.

"he was told to by a local minister. It was supposed to stop the devil from taking his spirit. I don't think they realised it would turn him into a devil".

"no shit!" Michael replied back, with an annoyed tone in his voice.

"why is there a house carved on the stone?".

Jay frowned "Geoff built the house from scratch. When we first moved here, there was a crumbling old cottage here. So, he had it pulled down and had this one built in its place, it was his pride and joy".

"is there any significance in the skull and crossbones on there?" I asked.

"the attic was his favourite room in the whole house, that's where he had his personal library. I was never aloud to go up there, the door was as far as I was allowed to go". She replied.

I pointed down to the stone. "so, we are going to have to dig him up. What is it we are looking for?".

"whatever is with him down there, it will be something from myself and Toby. We won't know until you get down there".

I looked around for a shovel or something that we could dig with. The best we could find, was a couple of large sticks. I handed one to Michael and we started scraping at the dirt. It moved easily and within minutes we had dug a relatively large hole.

We hadn't dug too far, as we were down to our knees in the hole. There was a loud thud, as my stick hit the ground. This made us speed up a little. We started scraping with our hands, scooping the soil away. Eventually we revealed a tatty coffin. The wood deteriorating and flaking, the moisture in the ground slowly eating away at it.

We cleared the remainder of the dirt and worms of the lid of the coffin. To the right side of the lid, I could see, what was left of the lid handle. I took hold of it and tugged. The smell of putrid flesh hit me square in the face. Inside the coffin, laying silently, but in a state of severe decay was Geoff. He was almost virtually bones and clothing.

Slowly, I opened his jacket, to reveal the inside pocket. carefully, I put my hand inside. My fingers touched a small box, so I wrapped my hand around it and pulled the box out. It was a small trinket box.

The sides were plain wood. But the top was special. Across the long Edge were beautifully carved, patterned loops. In the centre, were odd Looking symbols. I was unsure what this meant, and I was worried at how serious this was becoming. I lifted it up and passed it to Michael.

He started looking at it and then placed it on the floor, not wanting to touch it any longer than he needed too. I found the same in the other breast pocket. a similar trinket box, with identical symbols across the top.

Knowing Michael wasn't keen on touching the box, I placed it onto the floor by the side of the grave and proceed to climb out.

I sat on the edge of the grave and picked up one of the boxes to examine it. On the front was a small keyhole. The other box had the same. We would have to smash them open to see what they contained. "you won't be able to open them, without the keys" Jay calmly told us.

Michael found this funny and started to laugh. "they are small wooden boxes, why not just smash them on the gravestone to open them?".

"they are protected. That's what the symbols mean. You have to have the keys. That's the only way to open them". She replied.

I looked up "where the hell are, they then?".

Jay raised her arm, pointing at the carving of the skull and crossbones on the gravestone. "in the attic".

Michael and I both thought the same, but it was him that said it first.

"your saying, we have to go up there?".

I could see the sorrowful look on Jays face.

"that's his room. If the keys are in there, I cannot help you. I'm bound not to go in there. Anything else I can help with, but not go in there, that's why I need you to help".

Michael became very sarcastic "that's not a problem. We will go in on our own and you can stay outside the room". That didn't go down too well in my books, we were trying to help, and he could cause a problem if he upsets her. Jay hadn't noticed it.

"you don't have to worry about that. If there are any problems up there, go down to the kitchen and stay there. You will be safe".

"why is that? What is so special about the kitchen?" I asked.

"just as I am bound, not to go into his library, he is not allowed into the kitchen. That was one of the rules, we had in our lives and so it has continued after our death".

Michael gave a sigh of relief "that's good then, if he starts on us, we can run down to the kitchen and hide until he goes away".

Jay shook her head "that won't work. He has a perseverance that is second to none. He will wait until you either leave the kitchen or die. Which is what he wants. He wins either way".

"oh great, so basically we are fucked, no matter what we do" Michael screamed.

"no, its not that bad. If needed, I can divert his attention away. Maybe long enough for you to find the keys and get back to our graves. The graves and the kitchen are the only safe places" she replied.

I looked at Michael "grab something hard, in case we need to bash our way around in there".

He grabbed a stick and started to swing it around his head "not sure this will help against a ghost, but who knows". He laughed.

I approached Jay "we will do what we can. We will call for you or get down to the kitchen".

Jay then began to disappear. "just call for me and I will be there" she replied and with that she was gone.

We cleared the holly bush and began to head towards the house. The moon had been covered by a thin layer of cloud. Luckily, we could still see the stones without the use of the torch. The last thing we wanted to do, was broadcast that we were on our way back.

We arrived at the back door. I looked at the doorknob. There was nothing oozing out of it, it was clean and warm.

Michael then bent down and inspected everything around the door. He started to look through the keyhole and into the kitchen.

"do you see anything?" I asked.

"I can't see much, it's too dark".

"sod it. Lets just get in there, it's getting cold out here. It's got be warmer inside, I think I would rather die in the warm than freeze to death out here in the cold". I replied.

Michael grabbed the handle and slowly pushed it down, so as not to make too much noise.

The door gently opened, and we were amazed to see the kitchen was as it was before. The warm glow throughout, food on the table and everything was clean and tidy.

Michael grabbed hold of, one of the big copper sauté pans that were hanging up and started swinging it above his head. "do you think this will do any damage, if needed?" he asked.

"do you really think, that's going to stop Geoff from getting you, you berk. He's a ghost, nothing we have will hurt him, apart from finding those keys" I replied.

"well if it shows him, that I'm not scared of him, I may as well give it a go".

I had no choice but to humour him. If it made him feel confident enough to get what we needed, then I wouldn't stop him.

'go for it, if he comes, you knock him for six" and I laughed.

As Michael practiced his batting arm, there came a tapping at the door, that led into the hall. Michael suddenly froze.

'there is something tapping on this door".

I walked over to the door and placed my ear against its wooden panels.

"you are right Michael, there is ". I wasn't sure exactly what it was, but we were soon going to find out.

I grabbed the handle of the door and turned. The tapping stopped. As the door opened, I stumbled backwards with fright and I gasped for air.

"what is it?" Michael called.

"you do not want to see this" and quickly slammed the door shut. I pushed my back against the wall and slid down to the floor. I knew, I had to prepare Michael for what he was about to see.

"you are not going to like this" I called to Michael. He had continued to swing different copper pans around. It was as if he were trying each one and seeing which one, he would be most comfortable with.

"Mike" I shouted. "snap out of it!".

"sorry" and he walked over to me.

"so, what was it knocking on the door?" he asked.

"promise me that you won't freak out and do a runner?"

"ok, I won't" and he stood next to me.

I clambered up off the floor and took a step towards the door. "are you ready to meet Toby?" I said and pulled open the door.

At the sight, Michael promptly fainted. His heavy body collapsing and hitting the floor.

Toby's body was dangling in front of the door. His lower legs hitting the door as he was swinging from side to side. Blood was dripping onto the floor, creating a large pool of blood that was creeping towards the kitchen.

We were seeing a playback. This was the moment after Geoff threw him of the landing. It was the same as what Jay had shown me, only from a different angle.

Michael started to come round. I leaned over to him and patted his cheeks a few times, in an attempt to bring him round quicker.

He shook his head and tried to get up. He couldn't quite muster enough energy. "sit here for a minute. Don't try to stand up".

He listened and stayed sitting on the floor. "was that? ". "yes, it was him, it was Toby". I replied.

After a few minutes, Michael was talking fine, and he felt good. He tried to stand up again, this time with success. He propped himself up when he reached half height, paused for a second, then pushed himself off the door and stood up straight.

"that's better" he says, brushing the dirt off his backside.

"sorry mate, I did try to warn you" I said feeling sorry for him.

"that's ok, I should have expected it really, after what has happened so far this evening".

He started to walk around the kitchen talking to himself. To start with, I couldn't make out what he was saying. After his second lap of the centre table, I made out what he was saying. He was saying he was fine. Then he ran directly to the sink and threw up.

"we need to get moving, he is playing with us. he is trying to stall us from getting the keys". I called.

"ok I'm fine" and he took a sip of water, swilled it around his mouth and spat it into the sink. Followed by another sip which he swallowed.

"right, I'm good. Let's go" and he made his way to the door. I held out my arm to stop him from going any further.

"good. I think we have gone back to when Geoff murdered Jay and Toby, so we need to be careful. Keep your eyes open. The first sign of anything, let me know".

I opened the door. Toby was still hanging in front of the door; his legs had stopped swinging. We carefully brushed past Toby's body, trying our hardest not to disturb him.

"I don't like this".

"don't panic. Just remember what Jay told us. if anything goes wrong, get back here as quick as possible".

"right, got it" he replied.

I took a step further into the hallway, checking in every direction possible as I went. Michael was following right behind me, double checking everywhere I had already looked.

As we were walking, I had a suspicion that we were being watched. We cleared the bottom of the staircase and turned to walk up the stairs. I stopped and Michael walked into the back of me.

My gaze was at the top of the stairs. There was something there, it wasn't quite clear, but It was square in shape. We stood staring for what felt like an eternity, when a strange blue glow started coming from the bedroom I had seen in the vision, Jay made me see.

It proceeded to move along the landing towards the object. Then it stopped directly over it. It was a gravestone. It wasn't Jay or Toby's. then the lettering came into view. It was Steve's. on the front it read STEVE. R.I.P.

"we can't believe what it says. He's trying to get to you Michael".

Michael was biting his nails, whatever Geoff was doing, it was starting to work on him. I must have turned round just in time. As I did, the stone lifted off the floor.

From somewhere upstairs a voice shouted down to us.

"GET OUT!" and the stone came hurtling towards us. I jumped at Michael and pushed him out of the way, as the stone crashed to the floor, right where we were both standing.

Splinters of wooden flooring flew in all directions.

"That must have been Geoff" Michael said comically.

"you think" I replied.

I looked at the stone. It hit with such force, that it had buried itself deep into the floorboards.

In a blink, everything went back to the way it was before. All the light had gone, and we could feel the dust in the air, and Everything was calm.

"shit, that was close. I think he is trying to split us up".

"that is not going to happen" Michael shouted out, up the stairs. There was still a strange atmosphere around the house, but at least for the time being, he wasn't here with us. he had probably gone back to his realm to continue torturing Steve and Tony.

Michael rose from the floor "I think we need to get up to that attic as quick as possible". Michael was busy brushing the dust off himself. I looked up at the top of the stairs, to see if there was anything that could stop us getting to the attic. I took out the torch and clicked the button. The battery was completely dead. In frustration, I threw the torch to the ground.

Jay must have been watching us. when the torch stopped rocking in the corner where it was tossed. The yellow glow returned. It started in the doorway of the kitchen and gradually moved throughout the ground floor and up to the landing.

With the light brightening, we could see that it was clear, so, we started to climb the stairs.

After some laboured steps, we had reached the top. Michael then grabbed the back of my jacket and tugged for me to stop.

"what is the matter with you now?".

"look at the steps where we were standing". I turned and looked down the stairs. On every step, in the exact spot we had placed our feet, were footprints of blood. The stairs must have been like a sponge. It had to of been soaked with blood and every time we took a step; the blood would come to the surface. What was more alarming, was that the blood did not soak back into the step. It stayed there. The strong smell of iron wafting up from the steps confirmed with me that it was definitely blood. But whose was it?

"he's trying to wind us up again. Just keep going".

"no problem, I'm ok, I'm with it. Let's go" and within another step, we were both on the landing, facing the room that led to the attic. I could see the door clearly, but I could also see something dripping off the handle. As we got closer, we were able to confirm with each other, that it was the same gunk that was on the outside of the kitchen door leading to the garden. We walked into the room, closer to the door. Whatever the stuff was, it looked fresh. It was still dribbling off the handle and slopping on to the floor.

"so! Do you fancy touching that?" asked Michael in disgust.

"no, you're alright" and I dipped my hand into my right trouser pocket and pulled a hanky. "this will do the trick" and started to wipe the handle clean.

With the handle clean, I threw the hanky to the floor. A reached back for the handle, I could feel heat coming from it. "careful, he might have rigged it or something" Michael pleaded.

"oi!" came a voice from behind us and I almost jumped into Michaels arms. We thought it was Geoff, but when we turned, we shocked to see that it wasn't, in fact it was Tony.

"and where the fuck have you been?".

"more to the point, where the fuck has you been? One minute, you're there and the next, you had run off" Michael shouted back.

Tony shrugged his shoulders "sorry, I saw something, and it spooked me out, so I pegged it" he replied.

"I ended up in this room and I stayed there until I heard you two coming up the stairs. Have you managed to find Steve yet?".

"no, but we will".

Michael suddenly released his true thoughts "don't be daft. Didn't the gravestone tell you anything? Steve's dead".

"that didn't tell me Steve was dead. As I said before, it is him trying to wind us up and it's working on you pretty well" I shouted back. "now that we have Tony back, we stand a bit more of a chance".

Tony walked into the room and joined us at the door to the attic.

"why are we going up there for?". Tony asked.

I turned to face a concerned Tony. "we found out a few things about our mad host and it would appear that the answers to the problem, are up there".

I reached for the handle again and as before, I could feel the heat. It felt hotter. Fortunately, the heat was just about bearable, and I took hold and turned the handle.

As the door opened, the heat in the handle vanished. All signs of the slime had also gone, even off the hanky, which was lying on the floor. The thought of picking it back up made me queasy, so I left it where it lay.

'so, who fancies going first then?" I asked.

We all looked up the small, narrow, spindly staircase into a strangely lit room. From where we were standing, we could not make anything out.

No one replied, which was something I half expected, so I took the first step.

"we must be mad" Tony mumbled as Michael joined me on the stairs.

"it's got to be done" Michael replied as he followed me into the unknown.

Suddenly there was a strange noise from all around us and then tony screamed.

Both me and Michael turned to see Tony's feet being dragged along the landing

"bring him back you bastard" Michael shouted and ran out towards the landing. I followed by jumping from where I stood, clearing four steps before thumping hard on to the floor. As I landed, a shockwave of pain raced up my leg. I ran and caught up with Michael on the landing, just as the door to the room Steve vanished in, slammed shut.

"get after him" I cried and raced down to the room.

I grabbed the handle, which was piping hot. I didn't care. I wasn't prepared to lose another friend to that thing.

As I took hold, I could hear my skin sizzling from the heat, it started blistering and then smoking. The pain was intense, but I had to push it out of my mind for Tony's sake. I pushed the door and it flew open so fast, that I thought it would go through the wall and into the neighbouring room.

At the far end of the room, I could see Tony, but he looked different from earlier. He was still. He just stood there with his hands up above his head. All I could hear from him, was a faint moaning. Although, it didn't sound like him at all. I was just about to walk over when Michael came running through the doorway.

"where is he?" he shouted.

As he said that, a voice returned that sounded familiar and it wasn't Tony's.

"you will not have your friend back in one piece" and with that, a piercing blue light, filled the room. I struggled to focus on Tony in the corner, still motionless and with his hands above his head. There was something else in the room with us. A dark fog was beginning to form next to Tony. I could only assume that it was Geoff.

"give him back Geoff" I called.

"you know my name, how clever of you. Not that it makes a blind bit of difference" he smirked.

With that reply, came what I could only describe as a ripping sound, followed by a wet popping sound.

Geoff was ripping Tony's body in two. His innards, flying out and scattering across the floor. Not a single sound came from Tony's mouth, as his poor body as spilt into two. So, I could only gather, that he had already been dead. After being mutilated so violently, Tony finally became still. Blood still pouring from the two halves of his body and flowing across the floor, creating a crimson carpet.

Geoff, by this time, had gone. Leaving Michael and I, facing the remnants of Tony.

"that's it. The fuckers had it now. I'm going to fucking kill him" Michael shouted, turning and starting to run back towards the attic.

I caught up with him and stopped him, just in time to see the door slam shut in front of us. I knew now that we were going to have one hell of a fight if we were going to get out of here with our heads still on our shoulders.

Chapter five

"please be careful" a faint voice echoed across the landing. it could only have been Jays. I could hear the sound of urgency and caution in her voice. She was standing next to the attic door.

"don't worry, I will".

"let's deal with this bastard for good" Michael shouted as he stormed into the room.

I held my arm out "wait, remember, we only need to find the keys. If we find them, then he may have no choice but to let us go. He won't want anything to happen to them".

"so, basically, we can hold them for ransom?" Michael questioned.

I smiled at him "hopefully, and if it works, we can get out of this shithole".

"sounds good to me" and he grabs the handle.

Again, the door opened with ease. The weird light was still there, and we started to slowly and quietly walk up the steps into Geoff's private room. The room wasn't that big, you could see every part of it, from one end to the other. Along the sides of the room, were bookshelves full of books and papers. Behind the books were various period wall coverings.

A few paintings and pictures were neatly hung here and there. The pictures were faded and barely recognisable. The paintings were bold in colour and looked new.

A couple of old oil lamps were dotted around the room. These had been lit and were casting flickering orange light on the walls and ceiling. Surprisingly, the room felt warm and comfortable in a worrying way.

In the centre, we could see a writing desk made of dark oak. It was open with writing equipment scattered about the writing pad. Placed on the top was a silver tray. On that was a small cut crystal decanter, with a dark coloured crystal stopper and a couple of tumbler glasses placed next to it.

We walked up to the writing desk. I noticed a funny musty smell and held my nose briefly. Michael watched me do this and did the same "it does smell a bit, doesn't it?".

I dropped my hand from my face. It wasn't the sort of smell; I would have expected from this room. It looked too clean and tidy or was this just a playback like before. Michael started looking at the pictures on the walls. I had no interest in them. All I wanted, was to find the keys and possibly the best place to look, was the writing desk. I let him browse the room.

He started taking books off one of the shelves and reading the spines.

He laughed "Christ, he read some boring books." And he held up a book titled 'WHEN A FLOWER DIES '.

I could honestly say, I had never heard of it before. It was fairly thick and would have taken an avid reader weeks of nonstop reading, to get through it.

He put it back and picked another, then another.

In the middle of the writing pad on the desk was a small piece of writing paper, half filled with words. Geoff had obviously started a letter to someone called Terence and for some reason, never finished it.

Maybe he started writing it, when his mind went over the edge and started his rampage of terror against Jay and Toby. Who was Terence? So, I picked up the letter carefully and started to read.

DEAR TERENCE.

DEAR FRIEND, YOU HAVE BEEN THERE FOR ME FOR A LONG TIME. EVER SINCE MY FATHER DIED YOU HAVE BEEN THERE AT A MOMENTS NOTICE. BUT I FEEL THERE IS ONLY ONE THING YOU CAN DO FOR ME NOW. I HAVE DISCOVEREDA FEW THINGS THAT WILL CHANGE MY LIFE FOREVER AND I BELIEVE THERE IS NO OTHER ACTION FOR WHAT I AM ABOUT TO DO. WE HAVE ALREADY TALKED ABOUT WHAT WE WOULD WANT DONE, IN THE MOMENT OF OUR DEPARTURE FROM THIS LIFE AND IT WILL NOW BE IN YOUR HANDS TO DEAL WITH. I'M SORRY BUT

That was all it said, I turned the paper over, half expecting there to be something written on the other side. All there was, was another strange symbol lightly etched onto the paper in pencil. I had seen it before on both the trinket boxes.

I placed the paper back down on the desk, slightly nudging it into roughly the same position it was in, before I picked it up. to the back of the desk, were a series of shutters and drawers. I started opening them to see what they were hiding. Most had nothing special, just the normal writing implements and things. Then I came to a tiny drawer with a flower carved into the front. I pulled, but somehow it was locked. There wasn't even a keyhole. This was one of these secret draws. There was a latch somewhere on the desk, that would unlock the drawer. But finding it was now the most important thing.

I started looking over the desk, opening the shutters and drawers for the second time.

I lifted up one of the shutters and to my surprise, I found the same rose carving on the inside of the compartment. I run my finger over it. I hardly touched it, when there was a click and I could hear the sound of something move in another part of the desk. When I looked, the little drawer with the rose carving on, had moved forward.

"yes!" I said.

"what have you found?" Michael asked. Skipping over to me and the desk.

"I think I may have found what we are looking for" and a leaned forward and took hold of the lip of the drawer and slowly pulled it towards me. Sitting in the middle of the drawer was a tiny metal hoop. On the hoop were two small keys.

"here they are "I called and immediately removed them from they're hiding place.

"good, lets get the fuck out of here!" Michael shouted.

We turned to walk out of the room and came face to face with Geoff.

"if you know what's good for you, you will put them back" he screamed. His voice piercing into my very soul. Sending a horrible chill down my spine.

"I'm sorry, but I'm not prepared to do that. Do you think, I'm that stupid, you have killed two of my friends and now you expect me to give you back the only thing that will stop you from killing us? I don't think so!".

"then you will suffer the same fate as your friends" and he began to walk towards us. I looked around and noticed the window was slightly open. I began thinking 'throw the keys out the window and run. We could pick them up once we get out of the room'. Jay's voice came into my thought "that's it, you have the keys. You need to get out. Throw them out the window. I can get them and take them to the kitchen'.

71.

That was a great idea. We had left the trinket boxes in the kitchen to keep safe. If Geoff couldn't go in there, that's the safest place for them to be.

"make one more move and these disappear" I said dangling the keys in his face.

"no don't!".

"then let us out of here!".

Oddly enough, I must have tapped into a secret power that we were totally unaware of. Geoff started to vanish into the now dimming light of the room. We could see straight through him. He took a step back and he was gone, but we didn't move, until I was sure he had gone. I gave it a few more seconds, threw the keys out of the window and then we started to walk towards the steps.

Just as we reached the frame of the door, Geoff's voice returned and was moving towards us "I will stop you!" he said.

That was enough for me. I turned to face the narrow stairs. Without thinking I started running, taking three steps at a time until I was standing in the room at the bottom. Michael was close behind. Within seconds we were standing on the landing, looking out into a black void. Everything was silent, apart from the sound of the wind rustling the leaves and branches. From downstairs in the lobby area, came a strange sound by the front door. We couldn't see clearly what it was. All I could make out was a swaying shadow. Something or someone was down there.

"what was that?"

"I'm not sure, but we need to get down there. That's the only way out to the garden" I replied and started to look around on the floor for something we could use.

Three feet from where we were standing, was the hanky that I used earlier on the door handle.

"grab that cloth, we can use it as a torch" and Michael bent over and retrieved it. I bent over and grabbed a piece of loose wood from the floor. Michael passed the cloth and I wrapped it around the end and tied it. I pulled a lighter out of my pocket and lit the cloth.

It was slow to light, but once it took hold, the flames progressed around the cloth lighting up the landing with a flickering orange light. I held the torch out over the bannister into the darkness.

In the hallway below us, was a small dark figure. It was too small to be Geoff.

"I think we will be alright" I said to Michael.

"what is it?" and he too leaned over the bannister to take a look.

"excuse me if I'm mistaken but isn't that the son?".

I blinked a few times to try and clear my vision and looked again. It was indeed little Toby. He was beckoning us down to follow him.

Michael twisted his head to look at me "do you think it's really him?".

I wasn't a hundred percent sure. "we don't really have much of a choice if we want to get out. We need to get down there" I replied. With that, we both started to walk down the stairs towards the front door.

"come quickly, my mothers waiting for you in the kitchen" Toby called out and he disappeared through the kitchen door.

We opened the door and there was Jay, standing by the porcelain basins.

She held up the keys "Toby retrieved them from the garden".

I was pleased for that. I wasn't too keen on wandering around the garden in the middle of the night looking for a set of microscopic keys. It would be like looking for a needle in a haystack.

"I take it, he tried to stop you?".

"he did, but I threatened to throw them out the window and he left. I wasn't going to mess around, so I threw them out anyway. I don't think he expected me to do it, so he hadn't planned for it". I replied.

"he did tell us; we won't succeed and that he will stop us" Michael added.

"yes, he may be able too. He has a power that I'm not too sure about, but we should be able to help" she said pointing to Toby, who was standing at the table picking at the still steaming food.

"I can help too" he said, spitting pieces of food across the kitchen.

"what is he likely to do?" Michael asked.

"I'm not too sure, but all I can say is to keep your wits about you. He is capable of anything" she replied, and she threw me the keys.

"we don't have much time; we must get moving. But where do we go now?" I begged.

Jay and Toby moved towards the back door "we have to go back to our graves, what we have to do next will only work there".

Michael skipped a few steps towards the table and grabbed another copper pan off its hook "good, lets get on with it" and he skipped to the back door.

Jay and Toby simply floated through. Michael grabbed the handle and thrust at the door.

"we must move quickly" Jay called back, and we could just see her and Toby moving across the grass.

Michael and I proceeded to follow. We had some courage, that I never knew before. Michael and I could see Jay and Toby. They were still walking in front of us, towards the willow tree. They paused, allowing us to catch up. "where is Geoff" I asked.

"at the moment, I cannot tell. But keep your eyes peeled".

Without warning, Michael jumped up into the air.

"what the hell is that?". We looked to our left towards the holly bush. We could see long, dark red, slimy tentacles like an octopus's slithering across the floor towards us. They were creeping over everything, touching and feeling everything, they came across.

Jay then saw them. "it's Geoff. Run!" she yelled out.

I ran full pelt into Michael and pushed him to move faster. He finally realised how important it was to move as fast as possible and he started running too. We saw them just in time. As we caught up with Jay, I looked behind me, to see the tentacles had reached the concrete path and realised that, we had a narrow escape.

Jay and Toby had reached the willow and parted the branches, to form a gateway through to the centre. We ran through and the branches dropped back into place.

Jay walked over to me "I saw Geoff try to get you, are you ok?".

Michael answered first, raising my concern for him. "I don't think so" he replied with laboured breathing. He wasn't the fittest of guys and he also had asthma, which didn't help when running like we did.

"take it easy for a moment. Sit down here and rest, he cannot get you in here". Toby said and he turned and point to the graves.

"thank god for that. I don't think I could go much further" Michael grasped as he sat down against the trunk of the tree.

"what now?" I asked.

"we need to get them boxes open, to see what he has in them". I agreed. I stood behind the gravestones, Withdrew the boxes from my jacket and placed them on top of Jay's gravestone. As soon as they made contact with the stones, we heard a shout from the house and the symbols started to glow bright red.

Jay looked out of the willow. "somethings wrong. The light has come back on in the attic again. I think he's up to something" and she walked through to the direction of the house.

Oddly, I felt completely defenceless without her here. What was Geoff up to? He had something up is sleeve, probably the reason why he hadn't managed to get us yet. Although it was a fairly calm night, there was a slight breeze. As I stood there staring at the boxes, the sound of the wind started to become louder. I could see the branches of the willow, start to dance. I looked at Michael, he was out for the count. As soon as he was comfortable, he fell asleep.

I walked over and started to shake him "Mate, you need to wake up".

He started stirring and he opened his eyes. "what is going on? has he gone? He asked and he raised his hand so I could help lift him off the floor.

"no. I think he s still out there. The attic light has come back on again, so Jay has gone to see what it is".

"ok. Are we still safe?". "yes, we are for now" I replied.

Suddenly the wind picked up. instead of gently dancing branches, they started to sway violently. we could hear it, forcing its way through every gap it came too. Every few seconds, we could see the house. The light flickering from the attic window could be seen clearly. Worryingly, there was something else in the wind. Michael stood at the edge of the willow canopy watching.

There was something in the wind. Every now and then I could see things moving in the air.

"do you reckon it's him again" Michael asked.

"I wouldn't be surprised" I, however, knew that it was him.

Suddenly it looked like we were in a storm. The branches were flying in all directions, we moved back, closer to the trunk of the tree. We placed ourselves between that and the graves in a bid to get some shelter.

Michael lifted his head to take a look. "what do you think Jay is up to?".

"I'm not sure. Probably fighting Geoff"

"well I hope she kicks his arse" he shouted towards the house. Then something flew through the branches and sliced across Michaels face. His cheek flapped open and blood began to pour out of the wound and down his face. He jumped up, placed his hand up to his cheek and he ran out of the cover of the willow and headed towards the house. The last thing I saw before the wind suddenly stopped and the branches came down, was Michael running past the back door.

Toby was nowhere to be seen and I was now on my own. I decided I would stay where I was until Jay returned.

I wasn't sure how long I had been asleep for. It was still dark when I woke, so it couldn't have been for long. I could hear Toby's voice coming towards me and sat up straight, as he walked through the branches.

"we don't have much time; we must act fast. My mother is keeping Geoff busy. You need to open the boxes now!" he pleaded.

"what am I supposed to do?" I questioned Toby as I picked up the boxes and foraged for the keys.

Toby wasn't sure, so, it was down to me to try and figure it out. I found the keys and held them up.

They were both identical, so I picked one and held it to the first box. I pushed the key into the lock and tried to turn the key. It moved a little, then stopped. No click and the lid wouldn't lift. I put the box down and retrieved the other. Placed the key into the lock. A bright blue light glowed from the symbol on the box and as I turned, I heard it click and the lid lifted.

Inside, lay a lock of blonde hair. A little confused, I closed the lid and placed the box down on the top of one of the gravestones. I picked up the other, chose the other key and inserted it. As I did, there was a howling scream from the house. "I don't think he's happy" Toby laughed.

"he knows he's finished" Jay replied as she walked through to us.

"so, what am I doing once I've opened these boxes?".

She walked over to my side. I picked up the first box and lifted the lid. She knew exactly what he had done and how to correct it.

"he took our hair!" she cried out.

I opened the other box to reveal a lock of dark hair. This must have been hers and the blonde was obviously Toby's.

"but these boxes just have hair in them. What is the connection?" I must have had a really stupid moment. Once she explained it to me, it all made sense. Geoff and this Terence guy must have researched some black magic or something and decided to use it against Jay and Toby. Each box had to hold each person's hair. This would lock them to the person that places the hair in the boxes after they had died.

"you must return the hair to us" she pleaded.

"how? You want me to dig your bodies up as well?".

"that won't be necessary. Take each lock of hair and place it on top of the right gravestone. My hair, my stone. Toby's hair, Toby's stone".

Now that made perfect sense and I was silly not to realise that before. I opened toby's box, which was still glowing. Picked out the lock of his hair and leant forward to his gravestone. I gently placed the hair down onto the stone. The glow on the box faded.

I turned to face Jay "is that it?" I asked and then noticed something had changed. Toby had gone. I turned back to the stone, just in time to catch the last strands of hair merging into the stone.

"Toby is free. After all this time, he can now rest".

"you won't win!" I spun on my heals, to see Geoff standing on the other side of the willow. His face a horrific scowl.

"sorry but it looks like we already have!" I shouted back.

"I was never interested in him. He means nothing. But my wife on the other hand, is mine. If I don't have her, then no one will. She will be trapped here forever". And he started to laugh. His laugh soon came to abrupt stop, when I placed Jays lock of hair onto the stone. He was that confident that he had won, that he wasn't paying attention to what I was doing with the box behind my back.

His laugh was echoing around the garden, then it suddenly stopped as Jay's hair melted away on her gravestone.

Jay turned and looked at me "thank you, I will see you very soon" and she faded out and was gone.

They were now free of Geoff. but Geoff was still standing there. Although his face had now changed. He was worried about something. His face started to glow, and his eyebrows raised to reveal a saddened face.

"I only wanted her forever!" he shouted. As he did, cracks started to appear all over his face. Red light shone through them. Then they started to bleed as the cracks became wider.

I almost felt sorry for him, but after what he did over the last hundred years, he was going to get what was coming to him.

I found it hard to tell whether he was crying or if the tears I thought I could see were actually blood.

I took a step towards him, not caring for my own safety. "what have you done with my friends? You bastard" I shouted. He didn't hear me. The pain he was now receiving, had taken over.

His arms became outstretched, as if he were trying to grab me. I made sure he couldn't, by taking a step backwards, almost stumbling as I did. The wind had picked up again and I could see fragments of the house flying around the garden. It was breaking up.

I felt a sudden surge of energy and wanted to run, but I was unable too. I had to stay, to make sure Geoff was gone for good. The adrenaline was coursing through me, that I hadn't noticed that a piece of wood had hurtled through the willow branches and entered my leg. I felt no pain, although I could feel it inside my leg.

Geoff's hands started to change. The thick dark red tentacles we had seen in the garden before started to sprout out of his fingertips. They swayed a little, then they dropped, lifeless.

"where are my friends?" I asked one more time. I briefly saw his eyes look directly look at me. His mouth wide open and pouring with blood. I could see his throat pulsing, as his life was leaving him.

"nooooooo!" and his body slumped to the floor in a heap.

The wind stopped. I could hear things falling to the ground around me. I hadn't got the answer I wanted, but I was sure that he was now gone for good.

As I watched, his body convulsed once, then it started to blister and bubble. Then more shockingly, it started to melt.

Inside his clothing, his body started to turn into bright red fluid. It started to spread across the floor and headed towards me. I took a sidestep and watched it soak into the ground, until it was gone. Nothing remained except his clothes.

It was time for me to go. I started to walk back towards the house and stay in the kitchen. Although the house now looked partly demolished. I felt that would be the best place to hold up until the morning.

Once inside, I sat down beside the kitchen table and fell asleep. It didn't last long. Something was outside. I could see beams of light illuminating the garden. I found what energy I could and rose from the floor and shuffled out to the hallway and the front door. Everything had changed. The wallpaper was pealing. Dust lay everywhere and the front door was yet again hanging off its hinges and poking out from the floor.

As I approached the doorway, I could see where the lights were coming from. It was a police car. Its two occupants were walking towards our car. The pain in my leg was too much and I began to slow down my pace. They opened the car door and a leg dropped out. 'Who was in the car?' I thought. As I cleared the doorway and stood on the steps, I swore I could hear Jay's voice. 'I will see you again, check your pocket' she said. Then tiredness kicked in again and I collapsed to the floor just yards from the police car.

When I woke, I was laying in hospital. I lifted my arm to wipe my head and a searing pain ripped up my arm. I looked to see; I had a drip in place. Not happy with being a pin cushion, I slowly pulled the needle out and dropped it to the floor. I breathed a sigh of relief. Through the window, the sun was shining through. I was safe. Then I was hit with the question, 'who was it sitting in the car? '. I looked above my head and found the call button, I pressed it, then relaxed my arm.

Then I remembered the last thing Jay said to me before I collapsed. She said to look in my pocket. I looked to my left at the locker. My clothes were neatly folded and placed in a cubby hole next to my bedside. I reached in and started rummaging through my jacket. I could feel in the inside pocket, a piece of paper. I withdrew it and unfolded it. All there was, was one sentence.

TELL YOUR TALE, FOR YOUR FUTURE.   JAY

"you made it then bud" came a voice next to me. When I turned my head, at first all I could see was a bandaged face. Then I realised it was Michael. I was so relieved. we both lay there, talking about what had happened. The police had been and questioned Michael and cleared us of any wrongdoing, even though two of our friends were still missing.

The nurse came into the ward. I had to do a double take. At first glance I didn't recognise her face. I blinked and looked again, straight into the eyes of Jay. Only it wasn't her. This woman's name was Ellen.

Over my time in the hospital, Ellen and myself became very good friends. We talked all the time, at first, she would visit on her breaks, then as time went by, she was visiting on her days off and coming with me to my physiotherapy appointments. My leg never really healed properly, but I managed ok.

After a few months, I was discharged from hospital. Ellen and I got married, with Michael as my best man.

I was still unsure on whether to write about that night. I was scared of what Tony and Steve's family would say. Ellen finally persuaded me to do it, so I contacted Steve and Tony's relatives and after some talking, they agreed, and this is the end result.

To finish, Ellen is pregnant, and it looks like we are going to have a little boy. Everything was good, until Ellen scared the living daylights out of me. After running it through my head a number of times and talking with Michael. I understood and was happy with what she said, although it still felt a little weird.

While we were at a scanning appointment, someone asked if we had thought of any names. I was happy with any name as long as he was healthy.

Ellen just smiled "yes. Toby".

THE END

Printed in Great Britain
by Amazon